Terence

Harold

James

Duck

Toby

Gordon

Douglas

The Fat Controller

EGMONT

We bring stories to life

This edition published in Great Britain 2014
by Dean, an imprint of Egmont UK Limited
The Yellow Building, 1 Nicholas Road, London W11 4AN
Illustrations by Robin Davies and Niall Harding

Thomas the Tank Engine & Friends™

CREATED BY BRITT ALLCROFT

Based on the Railway Series by the Reverend W Awdry
© 2014 Gullane (Thomas) LLC. A HIT Entertainment company.
Thomas the Tank Engine & Friends and Thomas & Friends are trademarks of Gullane (Thomas) Limited.
Thomas the Tank Engine & Friends and Design is Reg. U.S. Pat. & Tm. Off.

HiT entertainment

ISBN 978 0 6035 6484 0
46819/6
Printed in Singapore

Thomas'
Wonderful Word Book

Based on *The Railway Series* by the Rev. W. Awdry

CONTENTS

the station

the farm

Welcome to my Wonderful Word Book! As you look through it, you can discover new words, enjoy spotting opposites and shapes and practise counting and telling the time.

Look out for Bobo the Clown who is visiting the Island of Sodor and enjoy the fun quiz at the end of the book!

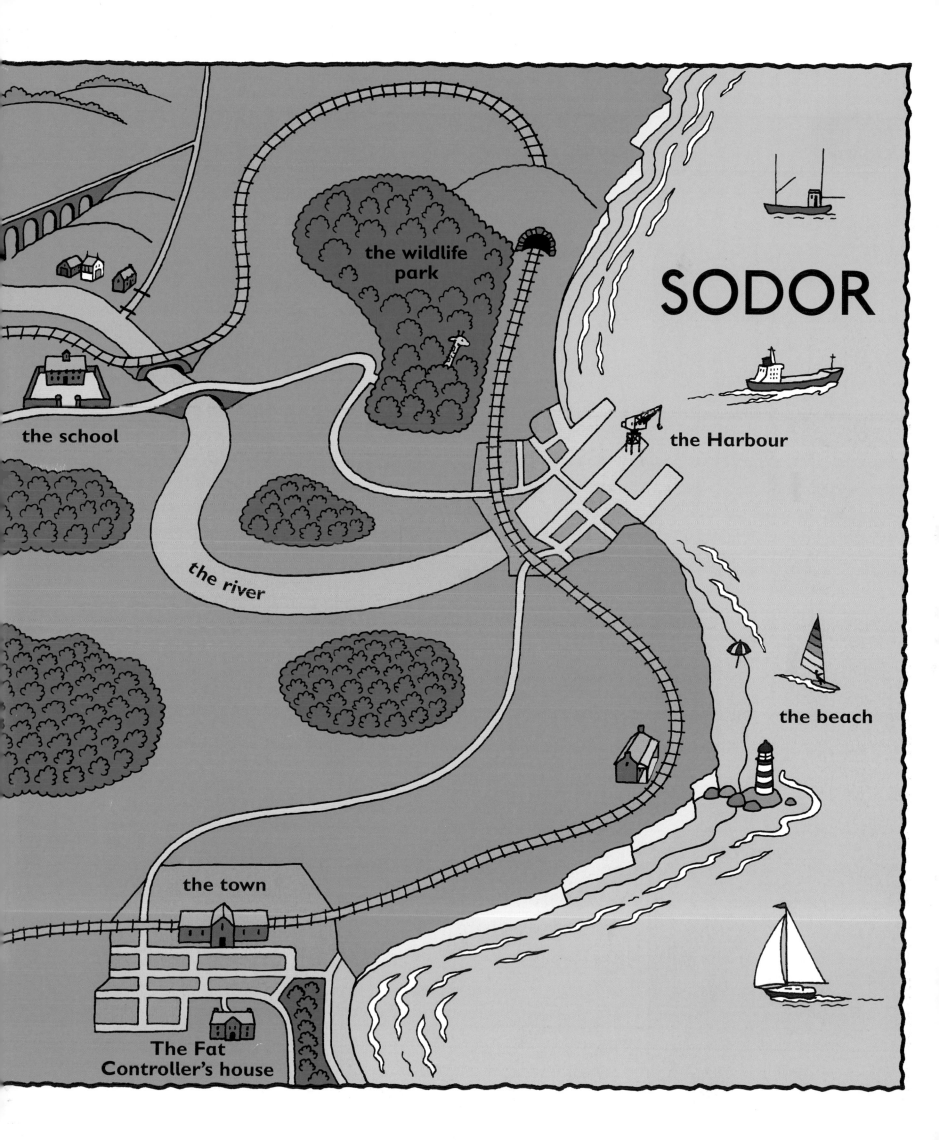

AT THE STATION

water tower

Duck

coal bunkers

Edward

siding

trucks

turntable

points

Toby

roof

James

signal

buffers

signal box

rails

Annie

Clarabel

BOBO

Annie

road

red bag

brown
teddy bear

pink bucket
and spade

brown
suitcase

green bin

ON THE PLATFORM:

shop

Snacks/Drinks

OPEN

newspaper kiosk

ben

Station
master

parcels

FRAGILE

buggy

coal

Driver

1

platform

Guard

The Fat
Controller

Porter

COLOURS

waiting room

clock

ticket office

TO PLATFORMS
2, 3 and 4

passenger

carriage

Annie

luggage trolley

family

brown briefcase

green flag

yellow umbrella

blue parcel

grey pigeon

MONDAY

The Mayor gives The Fat Controller a medal for his work on the Railway.

TUESDAY

Harold flies to the Harbour.

WEDNESDAY

The Fat Controller is busy in his office.

THURSDAY

James breaks down in a tunnel.

FRIDAY

Percy gets a new coat of paint.

SATURDAY

Percy takes passengers to the town.

SUNDAY

Thomas takes children to the seaside.

a for ambulance

b for Bertie

c for camera

d for dog

e for elephant

f for fire engine

g for garage

h for hose

i for ice-cream

j for jacket

k for kitten

l for ladder

m for motor bike

n for nest

o for orange

p for picnic basket

q for queen

r for rainbow

s for sandwich

· ON A PICNIC: LETTERS ·

t for tree

u for umbrella

v for van

w for wheel

x for xylophone

y for yoghurt

z for zebra

hamster

crayons

dinosaur

pirate hat

Thomas book

AT THE SCHOOL

blackboard

globe

paint brushes

paintings

Spring

computer

teacher

chalk

register

desk

drum

books

toy car

fish food

tambourine

recorder

Summer   Autumn   Winter

play house

window

doll

blocks

cupboard

train set   table

chair

mask   crown   cowboy hat   dressing-up box

aeroplane

pen

jigsaw piece

jigsaw

goldfish

apple

17

IN THE WILDLIFE PARK

buffalo

polar bear

penguin

kangaroo

elephant

hippopotamus

flamingo

tiger

rhinoceros

WildLife Park

camel

ticket office

school party

18

policeman

telephone box

motor bike

washing line

traffic lights

20

AT THE TOWN STATION

factory

park

playground

petrol station

carwash

statue

cinema

SQUINT & CO.

Mr. Bun

FOOT and Co

lorry

Annie

1

platform

steeple

town hall

house

church

fire engine

driveway

car

shops

van

Dan D. Lion & Son

Eat CHEESE

coach

TOYS B US

police car

road

street light

pavement

truck

petrol pump

aerial

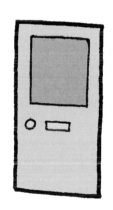

door

swings

pair of glasses

ON THE BUSY RIVER

aqueduct

sail

Bulstrode

yacht

river bank

dinghy

BULSTRODE   fender

police boat

POLICE

school

children

playground   wall

22

flag pole

sailing club

lock keeper's cottage

lock

canal

life belt

slipway

rubber dinghy

barge

motor boat

fishing rod

float

paddle

canoe

swans

tent

net

fish

oar

picnic basket

angler

rowing boat

fence

ducks

sleeper

23

Can you see . . .

RED Bertie?

an ORANGE jumper?

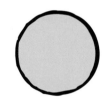

a YELLOW sun?

a GREEN flag?

a BLUE balloon?

AT THE FUNFAIR:

24

COLOURS

Can you see . . .

PURPLE flowers?

a BLACK hat?

BROWN coconuts?

PINK candyfloss?

WHITE Harold?

· IN THE COUNTRYSIDE ·

forest

corn field

Bertie

farm

grass

country lane

kestrel

cows

tunnel

badger

hedge

fox

mountain biker

Clarabel

sheep

rabbits

bird's nest

workmen

track

26

piglet

thrush

lamb

bull

cockerel

· BUSY FARM LIFE ·

Terence

farm house

pigsty

stable

cat

boots

axe

milk churn

horse

straw bale

farmer

goat

cattle grid

hedgehog

haystack

ewe ram

barn

hen house

barrel

log

chicken

Trevor

farm truck

pond

ducks

cows

calf

robin

sheepdog

donkey

chicks

sparrow

SEASONS: SPRING AND SUMMER

SPRING

James rides through the farm in the pouring rain.

SUMMER

Percy waits in the Harbour. It's lovely and sunny there.

SEASONS: AUTUMN AND WINTER

AUTUMN

The school children wave at Thomas as he goes by. It is getting colder and the leaves are falling off the trees.

WINTER

Henry watches the children playing. It's fun to slide about in the snow!

Can you see . . .

1 clock?

2 benches?

3 newspapers?

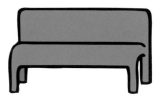

4 birds?

5 posters?

•PICKING UP PASSENGERS:

COUNTING

Can you see . . .

6 passengers?

7 mail bags?

8 suitcases?

9 parcels?

10 flowers?

35

crab

capstan winch

dolphin

mop

flatfish

· AT THE HARBOUR ·

beach

crane

buoy

container

ladder

bow

diver

container ship

fish market

fishing net

rope

ferry

oil tanker

tug boat

lifeboat

stern

seagulls

jetty

mast

sailor

funnel

fork-lift truck

lobster pots

Captain

Harbour master

life belt

anchor

porthole

flag

lobster

sun

cliff

café

OPEN

steps

ice-cream van

beach umbrella

sunhat

deck chair

children

puppet show

bucket

beach towel

sand castle

sunglasses

suntan lotion

spade

39

Can you see . . .

a CIRCLE?

a SQUARE?

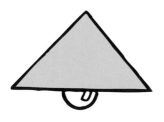

a TRIANGLE?

Can you see . . .

a STAR?

a DIAMOND?

a RECTANGLE?

OUT AND ABOUT: OPPOSITES

Up

Down

Open

Closed

Big

Little

44

Over

Under

Left

Right

Asleep

Awake

AT THE FAT CONTROLLER'S HOUSE

BEDROOM

STUDY

bedside lamp

wardrobe

curtains

book shelves

typewriter

bed

chest of drawers

cupboard

doors

light switch

clock

saucepan

plug socket

oven

lamp

jelly

kitchen table

rug

KITCHEN

HALL

BATHROOM

shampoo

mirror

picture

chair

tiles

taps

desk

bath

toilet

sink

BEDROOM

Harold

poster

blind

toy box

toys

coat stand

mirror

letter box

front door

telephone

floor tiles

LIVING ROOM

vase

cushion

sofa

carpet

vacuum cleaner

47

THE BIRTHDAY PARTY

I am 5

badge

party hat

bow

birthday present

pink shoes

juggling balls

birthday cake

clown

patio

plant pot

unicycle

steps

grass

dog

flower bed

lemonade

fairy cakes

jelly

sausage rolls

glass

jug

biscuits

cheese

table cloth

table

presents

socks

children

bouncy castle

shoes

balloons

plates

bowls

spoons

party
game

blanket

blue balloon

orange juice

crisps

candles

trumpet

7 o'clock

The engines wake up at 7 o'clock.

8 o'clock

Thomas picks up his passengers at the station at 8 o'clock.

9 o'clock

At 9 o'clock, James passes by the school.

10 o'clock

Harold is flying past the Lighthouse at 10 o'clock.

11 o'clock

It's 11 o'clock and Edward arrives with some parcels.

12 o'clock

The clock strikes 12 o'clock in the town.

1 o'clock

The Fat Controller has his sandwiches at 1 o'clock.

2 o'clock

At 2 o'clock, Terence is ploughing the field.

3 o'clock

Percy arrives at the Docks at
3 o'clock.

4 o'clock

The children wave goodbye to
Thomas at 4 o'clock.

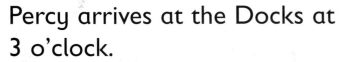

5 o'clock

It's 5 o'clock and Henry is going back
to the engine shed.

6 o'clock

The engines have a wash at 6 o'clock.

7 o'clock

Time for bed at 7 o'clock. Goodnight!

ANSWER: That's right,
Bulstrode was on the busy river.
(Page 22)

ANSWER: That's right,
the passenger was on the platform.
(Page 9)

Where did we find the following?

FUN QUIZ

ANSWER: That's right,
the fish tank was at the school.
(Page 16)

ANSWER: That's right,
the zebra was in the wildlife
park. (Page 19)

Where did we find the following?

ANSWER: That's right,
the boy was on the beach.
(Page 39)

ANSWER: That's right,
the candyfloss and coconut stall
was at the funfair. (Page 24)

ANSWER: That's right,
the man was on a picnic.
(Page 14)

ANSWER: That's right,
the sheepdog was on the
farm. (Page 42)

Thomas

Annie

Clarabel

Henry

Donald

Percy

Edward

Bertie